TOYS MEET SNOW

TOYS MEET SNOW

BEING THE WINTERTIME ADVENTURES OF

A CURIOUS STUFFED BUFFALO, A SENSITIVE PLUSH STINGRAY,

AND A BOOK-LOVING RUBBER BALL

BY EMILY JENKINS
PICTURES BY PAUL O. ZELINSKY

schwartz & wade books · new york

Lumphy is
a stuffed buffalo.
StingRay is a
plush stingray.
Plastic is
a rubber ball.
She can't help it
that her name
doesn't match her body.
They all belong to the Little Girl, but she has gone away on winter vacation.

It is the first snowfall

of the year.

"Why does it decide to snow?"
asks Lumphy.

"Because the clouds are sad and happy at the same time," says StingRay. She is more poetic than factual.

"No, it's what rain becomes when the temperature is freezing," says Plastic.
"I read about it in a book."

"Let's go out," says
Lumphy. "I'm curious."

"Yes," says StingRay.
"It's beautiful."

"Snow snow snow!" says Plastic,
bouncing. "I've read about it, but
I've never touched it!"

"I need a hat,"
says Lumphy.
He is often cold.

"I need a plastic baggie,"
says StingRay. She is
dry-clean only. "Poke me
some air holes."

"I don't need anything!" shouts Plastic.
She just goes natural.

And so, with no small amount

of

effort . . .

. . . the toys go out into the snow.

"Is that a different tree?" asks
Lumphy. "It looks like a different
tree than before the snow came."

"It's turned into a candy
tree," says StingRay. "It
tastes like peppermint."

"No, it's the same tree," says Plastic. "I recognize the branches."

"It's a blanket of peace over

"What do you think snow is, exactly?" asks Lumphy.

the world," says StingRay.

"No, it's frozen water," says
Plastic. "I read it in a book."

"I mean, what is a snow*flake*?"
asks Lumphy.

"A snowflake is a tiny ballerina,"
says StingRay. "If you look closely,
you can see it dance."

"No, it's just really tiny frozen water,"
says Plastic. "I read that, too."

It is

not

easy

to build

a snowman.

Snow angels are easier.

Lumphy finds icicles on a fence.

StingRay finds a puddle that has frozen solid.

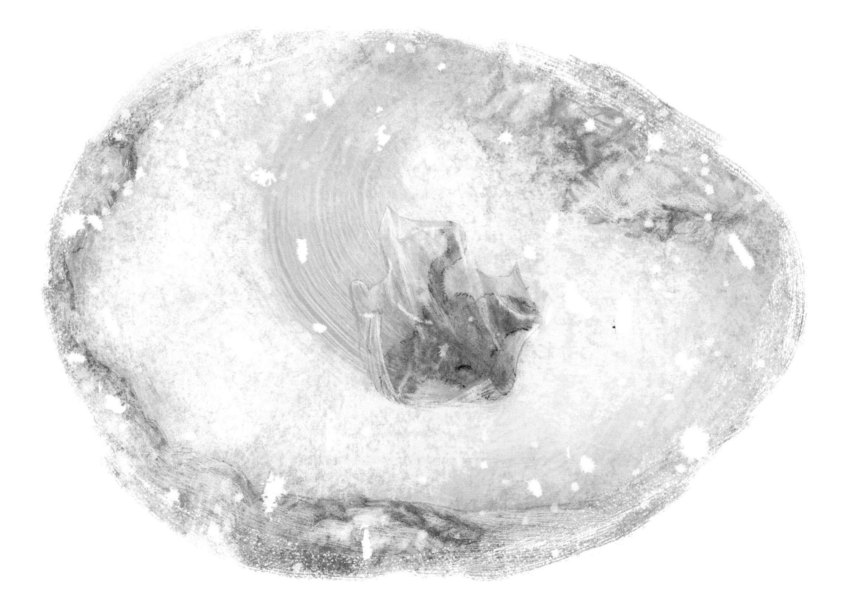

Plastic finds a forgotten sled at the top of a hill.

The day begins to fade.

"What is a sunset?" asks Lumphy.

"It's strawberry
syrup pouring
over the world to
make it sweet
before nightfall,"
explains StingRay.

Plastic doesn't say anything.
She is thinking.

"Brr. I'm cold," says Lumphy.
"My tail is wet," complains StingRay. Her bag is leaky.

"Snow snow snow!" cries Plastic. "I'm a strawberry-syrup sun in the snow!"

Inside, the house is dry and warm. Outside, the tiny ballerinas have made a blanket of peace over the world. The strawberry-syrup sun has gone down.

And yes, the world is sweet.

For Hazel and Ivy —E.J.
For Norma —P.O.Z.

Text copyright © 2015 by Emily Jenkins

Jacket art and interior illustrations copyright © 2015 by Paul O. Zelinsky

All rights reserved. Published in the United States by Schwartz & Wade Books,

an imprint of Random House Children's Books, a division of Random House LLC,

a Penguin Random House Company, New York.

Schwartz & Wade Books and the colophon are trademarks of Random House, Inc.

Visit us on the Web! randomhousekids.com

Educators and librarians, for a variety of teaching tools, visit us at RHTeachersLibrarians.com

Library of Congress Cataloging-in-Publication Data

Jenkins, Emily. Toys Meet Snow: being the wintertime adventures of a curious stuffed buffalo, a sensitive plush stingray,

and a book-loving rubber ball / Emily Jenkins ; Paul O. Zelinsky. — First edition.

pages cm.

Summary: While Little Girl is away on winter vacation, her toys, Lumphy, StingRay, and Plastic,

decide to go outside and learn more about snow.

ISBN 978-0-385-37330-2 (alk. paper) — ISBN 978-0-385-37331-9 (glb : alk. paper) — ISBN 978-0-385-37332-6 (ebook)

[1. Snow—Fiction. 2. Toys—Fiction.] I. Zelinsky, Paul O., illustrator. II. Title.

PZ7.J4134Whd 2015 [E]—dc23 2014010935

The text of this book is set in Tyrnavia.

The illustrations were rendered digitally.

MANUFACTURED IN CHINA

2 4 6 8 10 9 7 5 3 1

First Edition